Goosebumps®

PRESENTS

RETURN OF THE MUMMY

Adapted by Francine Hughes
From the teleplay written by Charles Lazer
Based on the novel by R.L. Stine

SCHOLASTIC INC.
New York Toronto London Auckland Sydney

A PARACHUTE PRESS BOOK

Adapted by Francine Hughes, from the teleplay by Charles Lazar.
Based on the novel by R.L. Stine.

ISBN 0-590-74589-1

Photos courtesy of Protocol Entertainment © 1996
by Protocol Entertainment.
Text copyright © 1996 by Parachute Press, Inc.
All rights reserved. Published by Scholastic Inc.
GOOSEBUMPS is a registered trademark of Parachute Press, Inc.

12 11 10 9 8 7 6 5 4 3 2   6 7 8 9/9 0 1/0

Printed in the U.S.A.   40

First Scholastic printing, September 1996

RETURN OF THE MUMMY

1

The pyramid shimmered in the heat. Its great triangle shape towered over me. Giant blocks of limestone were stacked up to the sky.

I felt tiny. Smaller than a speck of dust. Or should I say a speck of sand? After all, I was standing in the Egyptian desert. Pretty amazing.

Everything about the pyramids was amazing. Ancient Egyptians built them to bury dead kings and queens. The pyramid in front of me was built four thousand years ago. Amazing. Imagine something being four thousand years old.

I'm only thirteen.

So I felt tiny *and* very young standing in front of the pyramid. Just a regular kid visiting from the United States. Good old ordinary Gabe, with black hair and dark eyes. I should have been eating at a fast-food restaurant or hanging out at the mall. But I was in Egypt, looking at that amazing sight.

There wasn't much else to see. Sand, of course. A few scattered cars. Some tents pitched beyond them. The blazing hot sun.

It was only dawn. But it was already steaming hot.

I wiped the sweat from my forehead and hoped my cousin Sari didn't notice. Sari loved to tease me. She and my uncle Ben stood next to me at the entrance to the pyramid.

Sari looked as cool as anything. She didn't even squint in the glaring sunlight. Sari's exactly my age, but nothing bothers her. She is such a big know-it-all. Maybe it's because she's been in the desert tons of times with Uncle Ben. He works there a lot. He's a world-famous archeologist — and an expert on pyramids and mummies. It was the first time I had ever visited one of my uncle's digs.

My uncle was sure he was about to discover a lost tomb inside the pyramid. The tomb of Prince Khor-Ru, an ancient Egyptian prince. It was a secret dig — and I was part of it!

Pyramids are like dark underground mazes inside. They're full of secret passages and dead ends. I knew it was going to be spooky.

But I wasn't afraid.

"Imagine!" Uncle Ben exclaimed. "The tomb of Prince Khor-Ru is right in front of us!" He paused for a moment. Then he added, "At least I hope it is."

Sari grinned. She threw her long black hair over her shoulder. "If it *is* the tomb, you'll be even more famous, Dad."

Uncle Ben blushed. He likes to kid around, but he's really pretty shy.

Sari's not. Her black eyes lit up with excitement. "Let's hurry up and go inside."

My stomach lurched as I peered into the

small square entrance. Were we really going in there? What would it be like?

I gripped my flashlight. It would definitely be dark in the pyramid. Not too dark for my instant camera, though. The camera hung around my neck. I wanted to get everything on film. Maybe we would find the prince's mummy. I could pose with my arm around his shoulders.

"And there's really a mummy in here?" I asked, to be sure.

"Duh!" Sari said. "That's why they built the place, Gabe."

I knew that. I also knew that treasure was usually buried with kings and queens — and princes.

So there. I knew as much as Sari. It just didn't seem that way.

"Hey, what's this?" Sari asked. She leaned toward me, reaching for something. I pulled away, but not far enough.

She grabbed a small white bundle from my jeans' back pocket. "Ugh!" she cried. "It's a hand!"

2

For once Sari sounded surprised. Maybe even upset. But she held onto the hand and examined the tiny fingers.

The hand was wrapped in bandages. Some of the strips of material were coming loose. They were all brown and dirty from tar. In the old days, people used tar to glue things together.

"Give me that," I said, reaching for the hand. "It's my summoner."

Sari pulled the hand away.

"A summoner?" she repeated, laughing.

"That's right," I snapped. "It summons the dead. It's a real mummy's hand."

Sari laughed again. "You mean they sell mummy hands at shopping malls?"

"I bought it here — at the airport," I explained.

I would never have bought a mummy hand at home in a mall. Of course it would be a fake. I had bought this one from a real Egyptian standing near the baggage claim. I figured the hand had to be real, too.

Uncle Ben smiled at me. He patted me on the head. "I hope you didn't pay much for it," he told me. "Selling mummy parts is one of the oldest scams around here."

The Egyptian in the airport had told me the hand had special powers. I still believed him. I didn't think it was a scam.

Sari wasn't afraid of the summoner anymore. She held it up in front of her and screwed up her face as if the hand smelled bad. "Yech!" she said. "It's warm."

I grabbed it back. "Of course it's warm," I said. "That's because it communicates with the dead."

I smiled to myself. I had finally explained something to Sari.

Sari shook her head. "It's warm because it's been in your pocket," she insisted.

"Tell you what, Gabe," Uncle Ben said in a joking voice. "You can try out the summoner on Prince Khor-Ru." He stopped for a second. "But first we have to find him."

We all grew serious. This was important stuff.

"Here goes nothing," Uncle Ben muttered. He walked over to the pyramid entrance. He bent over, hunching down to get inside. Then he took a few steps and disappeared into the darkness.

Sari scooted in next. I patted the summoner for luck. Then I wiped my forchead one last time and followed Sari into the entrance.

In the passageway, the light dimmed quickly. The air turned cold. I peered into darkness ahead of me.

The place smelled old and musty. Soft sand covered the floor.

I flicked on my flashlight. I saw Sari crouched over, hurrying down the low, narrow tunnel. I knew Uncle Ben was ahead of her. Then I hunched down a little more and trailed after them slowly.

A few minutes later, the tunnel grew wider. The ceiling rose higher. Finally I could stand up straight.

I turned my flashlight on the stone walls. In one section I saw something etched into the smooth surface. I peered closer.

Pictures. Figures of people and animals.

"Gabe!" Sari called from farther down the tunnel. "Are you coming or not?"

"Wait a minute," I answered. "Let me get a photo of you and Uncle Ben next to this wall."

The two of them trudged back. Sari looked ready to kill me. She wanted to keep going. Uncle Ben brushed his hair back and fixed his collar. "Hope I look okay," he mumbled.

"You look fine," I answered. I was still holding the summoner. I laid it on the ground to take the picture. I gripped the camera with both hands.

"Now move a little closer to those pictures on the wall," I directed. "I want to get them in the shot."

Sari was disgusted. "Pictures?" she cried. "Those are hieroglyphics. They're four thousand years —"

"I know they're called hieroglyphics," I interrupted. "And I want them in the shot."

A wind suddenly swept through the tunnel. Sand swirled on the floor. I glanced down. Did the summoner quiver? Or was it my imagination?

Of course it was my imagination. The summoner wasn't moving. It couldn't. I squinted into the camera again. "Say cheese," I told Sari and Uncle Ben.

I sneaked another peek down at the summoner. It seemed to shake a bit. To stretch its fingers one by one.

I shook my head to clear my brain.

"We said cheese!" Sari complained. "Now take the silly picture already."

"Uh, just a minute," I said, fumbling with the camera.

Once more I tried to look at the summoner. Then I peered through the lens again.

"Gabe, it's very simple." Sari spoke slowly, as if I were three years old. "Just push the little button, and the picture pops out."

I shot her a nasty look. "I know how to do it!" I said.

"Could have fooled me," Sari teased.

I heard something creak behind me. I froze.

"Are you sure you can take a simple picture?" Sari went on.

Uncle Ben tapped his toe.

I heard more noises. A scraping sound behind me. Something moving across the sandy floor.

I wanted to turn around, but I had to take the picture right that second. Otherwise I'd look like a total jerk.

I snapped the shot.

"Now let's go!" Uncle Ben said. He and Sari turned to go farther into the tunnel.

"Wait!" I begged. I bent down and reached all around the dark floor. "Let me get my —" I didn't finish my sentence. I didn't have to. The summoner was gone.

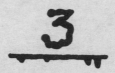

How could the summoner be gone? It couldn't have just walked away.

Could it?

I kicked the sand around. Maybe the hand was buried. No. It wasn't there.

I gave up and started to follow Sari and Uncle Ben. I didn't go very far. Something on the ground caught my eye. Something white.

I walked closer. I shined my flashlight on the spot. Light glinted off dirty white bandages and curled fingers. It *was* the summoner!

Did it walk that far by itself?

"Gabe!" Uncle Ben called. He was deep into the tunnel. "Come along now."

I shrugged. Maybe I kicked the summoner by accident. Or maybe Sari kicked it. It didn't really matter. I had the summoner back. And I wasn't going to say anything to Sari about losing the hand. It would just give her another chance to tease me.

I scooped the hand up quickly. I knew it was silly, but I really did believe the man in the airport. The summoner had power. Not the power to move on its own, of course. But some kind of power.

"Gabe!" Uncle Ben called again.

I looked down the tunnel. It seemed as if my uncle and Sari were waiting for me at the end of a long hall. "Gabe, we all have to stick together," Uncle Ben warned. "You have to remember that."

I knew he was right. The tunnels were dark and weird. And they went off in all directions. If I got lost, I'd never find my way out.

I stuck the summoner in my back pocket and scooted after my uncle.

My flashlight darted up and down the

walls. Strange shadows loomed on all sides. My footsteps echoed in the silence. They seemed to grow louder with every step.

I hurried along more quickly.

More pictures lined the tunnel. Hieroglyphics. My flashlight swept over them. Then I slowed down for a closer look. There was something about them ... something mysterious. Finally I stopped and stared at one of the panels.

I saw men in strange costumes. A snake hanging from a tree. An eye, wide open and staring. A sun, a moon, and stars.

I ran my hand along the carved outlines.

"Gabe!" Sari was suddenly standing behind me. "Let's go!"

I couldn't take my eyes off the pictures. Four thousand years old. Drawn by ancient Egyptians. Messages from another world.

"What do you think it means?" I asked.

Sari squinted. "It's all about death and the journey of the soul," she whispered.

Then she shivered. "Don't you feel death here?" she murmured.

I gazed at her, surprised. Was Sari spooked? Smart, know-it-all Sari? We followed the pictures down the tunnel wall.

More men in costume. They carried a dead person on a fancy stretcher. It had to be the prince. His eyes were closed. His arms were folded across his chest.

I swallowed hard. The prince didn't look much older than I am.

"Man, that's a creepy way to end up," I said. "I'd hate to be stuck in here all by myself. Wouldn't you, Sari?"

No answer.

"Sari?"

Still no answer.

I spun on my heels. Where was she? "Sari? Uncle Ben?" I called, louder.

Where did everyone go?

4

I wanted to run away. Every muscle in my body screamed: "Move!" But I didn't know which way to go. Should I turn around and try to go back and find the entrance? Should I go deeper into the pyramid to find Uncle Ben and Sari?

Thud! I heard a noise. It came from someplace farther down the tunnel. I took off quickly. My heart beat loudly in my chest. *Thump, thump.* The sound seemed to bounce off the walls.

A wave of heat rushed from my head to my toes. My hands began to sweat. I wiped them on my shirt and almost dropped the flashlight.

"Hello?" I shouted.

No answer. No more thuds.

I slowed down, listening. I crept along the tunnel. Then I turned into another passageway. And another. I flashed my light down a long corridor. Empty.

My heart sank down to my knees. I had lost Sari and Uncle Ben. There was only one thing to do. Go back. Find the entrance.

But now I was turned around. Which was the way out? Pyramids really were like mazes!

I froze in place, not sure where to go.

"Gabe? Gabe?" a voice called from far away.

I whirled around. Then turned again. Where was the voice coming from?

"Sari?" I cried. "Is that you?"

"Gabe?" The voice seemed to fade away. Sari and Uncle Ben were leaving me!

My legs trembled as I stumbled down a hallway.

"Sari?" I yelled at the top of my lungs. "Where are you?"

Silence. I strained to hear. Still nothing.

"Oh man," I whimpered. "I'm in trouble now."

Up ahead I saw two tunnels. Going in different directions. I stopped dead in my tracks. Which way?

Panic clogged my throat. Right? Left? I took a deep breath and started to the left.

"Sari?" I shouted. Dirt and pebbles clattered down from the ceiling.

I jumped.

The flashlight slipped out of my sweaty hand. It hit a stone on the floor. The light went out. I was in total darkness.

Blackness pressed in tight. My heart raced with fear. I felt as if I might pass out. I needed something to hold on to. Something to guide me back down the tunnel.

I reached out. I wanted to find a wall. A solid stone wall.

"Ah!" I shouted. There was no stone. No wall. Nothing but empty air.

I tripped into a dark hole. I tried to catch hold of a ledge. A rock. Anything. I threw my arms around wildly. They came up empty. And I kept falling.

"Oof!" I hit a sandy floor.

For a moment I didn't move. The wind was out of me. When I could breathe again, all I could do was groan.

Slowly I found some strength. "Help!" I finally shouted. "Help!"

I sounded scared. But alive. That was good. And I seemed to be fine. No broken bones. No major cuts. Now if only I could see.

Then I remembered I had another light. A pen light. I grabbed the pen from my T-shirt pocket and switched on the small beam.

I could just make out a ceiling high above me. Shadows flickered on the walls. They looked like figures swaying to music. I was in some sort of chamber.

How long would I be stuck in this creepy place?

A tingle of fear crept up my bare arm. The tingling moved up to my shoulder, then on to my neck and back down my arm.

It couldn't be fear. It felt too real.

I flashed the pen light on my arm. A huge spider sat on my arm. Hairy. Black. Ugly.

"Ahhhh!" I screamed.

I knocked the spider off.

"Whew!" I let out a deep breath. Just as quickly, I sucked in more air. What if there were more spiders? What if the chamber was one big spider pit?

Spiders could be creeping up my legs. Crawling into my clothes. Right now!

I shook myself from top to bottom. Then I jumped up and down, waving my arms. Finally I slowed down and caught my breath. Maybe there weren't any more spiders.

I flashed my pen light around the pit. Spiderwebs stretched from corner to corner. Then I spied something else. Some kind of object hanging on the wall.

The object was round and metal. It was the size of a dinner plate. It glowed with a soft golden light.

I moved closer. It was a lion's head!

"Whoa!" I said out loud. What was a lion's head doing there? In the middle of a pyramid? Did it mean anything? Something to do with Prince Khor-Ru?

I was so excited I forgot I was afraid. I'd discovered something, I felt sure. Something four thousand years old. Something made of gold!

I whipped out my camera and started snapping away. The flash lit the room again and again. I slipped the photos into my pocket. Now that I had some pictures, I wanted to look at the real thing.

I aimed my pen light at the lion's eyes. I leaned in close for a better look.

Too close. A snake swung out of the lion's mouth!

"Cobra!" I gasped.

My feet suddenly felt nailed to the ground. I couldn't move.

The deadly snake reached toward me. It hissed, loud and long. I saw its dark, hooded eyes. I watched its tongue dart in and out.

The snake jabbed forward suddenly, aiming for my neck. Its jaws snapped open.

"Oh!" I cried, jumping back. The snake

brushed past, missing me by an inch. But I wasn't safe yet. Another snake suddenly swung down from the ceiling.

"Snakes!" I screamed.

5

"That's no snake!" a voice above me said, laughing. "It's just a rope, you chicken."

"Sari!" I gasped.

My eyes followed the rope up to a hole in the ceiling. Sari and Uncle Ben peered back.

"Grab it, Gabe!" Uncle Ben called down. "Grab the rope!"

I clutched the swinging rope. It felt thin and frayed. Not too sturdy.

The cobra hissed behind me.

The rope would have to do.

"Get me out of here!" I shouted.

I wrapped the rope around my wrists and held on. Inch by inch, Uncle Ben and Sari pulled me up. I tried not to think about spiders or snakes or anything but getting out of the chamber.

I reached the top and scrambled through the opening. I was back in the tunnel above the chamber — with Sari and Uncle Ben. I've never been so glad to see them in my life.

Uncle Ben understood. He decided we'd seen enough for one day. He led the way out of the pyramid. Before we knew it, we were outside in the open air.

Sari grumbled as the three of us trooped to Uncle Ben's tent. Hours had passed since we started out. Night was coming.

The sun sets quickly in the desert. The temperature drops fast, too. Before long, moonlight beamed through the tent flap. Outside a chill wind blew sand in circles.

Inside the tent, I turned to Uncle Ben. "Oh! I almost forgot," I told him. "I have something to show you."

I pulled the pictures from my pocket. "I snapped these in the chamber," I explained.

Uncle Ben bent over the photos. "These

are fantastic, Gabe!" he exclaimed. "The lion's head is Prince Khor-Ru's sacred seal."

I sucked in my breath. "Is that true? Are you sure?"

"Look!" Uncle Ben said. He pulled out some textbooks and showed me a drawing in one of them.

I peered at the picture in the book. My heart beat excitedly. Uncle Ben was right. It was the same lion's head. The prince's seal. Right there in a textbook. I felt so proud!

"And you know what else, Gabe?" Uncle Ben continued. "The seal marks the entrance to the prince's tomb. That means *you* discovered the tomb!"

"He fell into it," Sari protested. "That doesn't count!"

"Of course it counts," Uncle Ben said. He slapped me on the back. "Tomorrow we're going back into the tomb."

So soon? I remembered the darkness. Being trapped in a maze. That lost, helpless feeling.

The spiders. The snakes.

"What about —" I began.

"Snakes?" Sari teased. "Won't your summoner scare them away?"

"We'll send *you* in first," I answered angrily. "That will scare the snakes. Probably even wake up the prince."

Uncle Ben shook his head. "Stop clowning around, you two," he demanded. "For your information, I've sent a work crew into the pyramid to clean out the snakes."

"There were spiders, too," I told him. "It was like a spider pit in there."

I reached around to my back pocket for my all-powerful summoner.

My back pockets were empty. So were my front pockets. I clapped my hand against my T-shirt pocket.

Empty.

I scrambled around the floor of the tent. Was it under the cot? Behind the tent flap?

No. It wasn't anywhere.

This time the hand had really disappeared.

"My summoner!" I gasped. "It's gone!"

"Maybe it's in another tent," Uncle Ben suggested.

"No way," I told him. "I had it with me in the pyramid. And then we came straight back here."

Uncle Ben scratched his head. "Well, you probably dropped it when you —"

"Became hysterical?" Sari interrupted, teasing again.

"Don't worry, Gabe," Uncle Ben went on. "The cleanup crew will find it. In the meantime, here's a little gift. It's a welcome-to-Egypt present."

Uncle Ben pulled a pendant out of his pocket. It hung in the air for a moment, swinging on a piece of string.

My uncle put the necklace in my hand. I stared at it. The pendant was round, made out of thick orange glass. It felt smooth and heavy.

"What is it?" I asked, holding the necklace up to the light. "Some kind of old glass?"

"No," Uncle Ben explained. "It's a clear

stone called amber. Amber is hardened sap from ancient trees." A glint came into his eyes. "Look inside the stone," he urged.

I peered at it closely. The amber gave off a golden glow. But there was something else . . . something inside.

"There's a bug in there!" I shouted.

"That's right." Uncle Ben nodded. "An ancient scarab beetle. It's been trapped in this stone for about four thousand years."

Four thousand years. The pendant was as old as the pyramid.

Sari tossed her long hair. "Great present, Dad. A dead bug!"

"It's totally cool," I whispered. Sari might not think the necklace was anything special. But I was happy. I couldn't believe it was mine.

Uncle Ben sat back on his heels, smiling. "I'm glad you like it, Gabe. Scarabs were very important to ancient Egyptians. They thought if you owned one, you could live forever."

I slipped the pendant around my neck.

"It's really four thousand years old?" I asked.

A soft voice outside the tent answered, "Yes, it's true."

"Knock, knock," the voice went on. "Dr. Hassad?"

The tent flap lifted. A woman stepped inside. Her straight black hair curled at her shoulders. Bangs brushed her forehead. Her dark eyes gazed around the tent.

She was as beautiful as an Egyptian princess.

Her gaze stopped at Uncle Ben. He stood up awkwardly.

"Dr. Hassad!" the woman said. She smiled brightly. "I'm so glad I found you."

Uncle Ben looked surprised. "Uh," he mumbled. "Excuse me. But do I know you?"

"My name is Nila Rahmad. I'm a reporter with the *Cairo Sun* newspaper."

"Hello," Uncle Ben said uncertainly.

"My newspaper heard that you have found the lost tomb of Prince Khor-Ru," Nila continued.

That was strange. How could the woman have heard about the dig?

Uncle Ben must have thought the same thing. He took a step back. "I don't know how the paper heard that rumor," he told Nila. "But we haven't found the tomb. Not yet, anyway."

Nila shot him a dazzling smile. "Even better!" she said. "I want this story. I want to come with you and write up the discovery step by step."

Uncle Ben hesitated. But Nila flashed him another smile, and he melted like butter. Not that I blamed him. Nila was great-looking.

"You should talk to my nephew Gabe first," Uncle Ben told her. "He's the one who discovered the door to the tomb. In fact, he's the only one who has seen it."

Nila whirled to face me. "Really? Are you an archeologist, too?"

I blushed, tongue-tied. But of course Sari spoke up. "Gabe's no archeologist," she said. She poked her elbow into my ribs so hard I tripped backward. "He's just clumsy. He fell into the tomb!"

Nila turned her gaze to me again. "Some of the greatest discoveries happened by accident," she said quietly.

Nila stuck up for me! That will show Sari, I thought. I did make a great discovery. Even if it was by accident.

Then a strange expression crossed Nila's face. "Odd," she whispered to me. "We're twins. I have a pendant just like yours."

She flipped a necklace out from under her jacket. It was the same shape, same color. Only hers looked empty. It didn't have a scarab in it.

Uncle Ben examined Nila's necklace closely. "How unusual," he murmured.

"It's prettier without the dead bug," Sari insisted.

Nila tucked her necklace back into place. "A scarab is good luck," she told me, smiling. "I hope my pendant isn't *bad* luck. Now, tell me, Gabe. What did you see in the pyramid?"

I held out one of the photos of the lion's head. "I took this picture."

Nila grasped it eagerly. "That's it!" she cried. "The seal of Prince Khor-Ru!" She held the picture tightly.

Uncle Ben raised his eyebrows. "I'm impressed by your knowledge," he said. "Not everyone knows the seal."

Nila shrugged. "I know a lot about ancient Egypt. I have studied it my whole life."

A strong wind suddenly swept through the tent. A large man had thrown the flap open. He carried enormous suitcases. And there were many more lined up behind him. Enough luggage for a queen.

"Where shall I put these, madam?" he asked Nila.

"Just leave them over there." As Nila waved her hand toward a corner of the tent, the Egyptian man spied my photograph. He stared at it and dropped the suitcases with a thud. His eyes filled with terror as he stepped in for a closer look.

"That photo, madam!" he exclaimed. "Surely you cannot —"

Nila hushed him. "It's nothing to worry about, Shafik."

Shafik pointed to the picture with a trembling hand. I had never seen anyone so frightened.

"No one must enter the tomb!" he cried. "It is cursed!"

"Cursed?" I repeated.

"Yes!" Shafik cried. "If you go inside, someone will die!"

6

"Enough!" Nila snapped at Shafik.

Shafik turned and bolted through the flap.

"What was that all about?" I asked. I still felt Shafik's terror. To be honest, I was scared, too. And we weren't even near the tomb!

Nila held the photo and showed me the writing above the lion's head. I didn't know what it meant. More hieroglyphics.

" 'Let me rest in peace,' " Nila read aloud.

My eyes opened wide. "You can read that stuff? 'Let me rest in peace.' What does it mean?"

"It's a warning," Uncle Ben explained. "It's supposed to scare off grave robbers."

"Sometimes tombs hold incredible jewels," Sari added in her best teacher's voice.

"I know that," I told her quickly.

"It is said that there are many jewels in the tomb of Prince Khor-Ru," Nila whispered. "More than one man has tried to rob his burial place."

"What happened?" I asked.

"The robbers were never seen again."

I gulped. Men had entered the tomb and never returned? Were they trapped? Lost forever in the twisty, winding maze?

Or did the robbers come face-to-face with the mummy?

The wind screamed outside. The tent flapped open. I shivered.

Sari didn't even make fun of me.

"There is a legend," Nila continued. "It has to do with three sacred words. *Kahru, Kahra, Kahri*. Repeat them three times, and the mummy will be awakened. He will seek revenge."

A nervous tingle crept down my spine. I knew it wasn't a spider. This was fear. Cold, dark fear.

"That is just superstition," Nila said in a normal voice. She flashed another smile. "And we are not superstitious. Right, Gabe?"

I woke up early the next morning. Harsh sunlight streamed through the tent flap. The heat was incredible. I fanned myself with the lion's head photo.

This was going to be the day. Warning or no warning, we would go into the tomb. I paid no attention to the nervous feeling in my stomach. I was going to be part of history.

"Prince Khor-Ru, here we come!" I cried as I leaped off the cot.

I scrambled into my clothes. After a quick breakfast, I met Uncle Ben, Sari, and Nila outside the pyramid.

"Everyone ready?" Uncle Ben asked.

We all nodded silently. Then we slipped through the entrance and into the pyramid.

This time I stuck close to the others. Uncle

Ben's lantern bobbed ahead of us. I didn't take my eyes off it as we traveled back through the tunnels. Back through the darkness. The sand. The close, stuffy air.

We were walking into the past. Leaving the present behind.

Uncle Ben led us in and out of passages. I don't know how he remembered where we had been before. But he did. He even found an open entrance to the chamber. We didn't have to lower ourselves into it by rope.

"Here we are!" he finally announced. "The chamber."

"Also known as the spider pit," I reminded everybody. I looked around for the creepy crawlies.

Nothing. The work crew must have cleaned them all out.

Then I felt it. A tingle on my neck. I brushed it away. A second later, it started again. The big hairy spider was back!

"It's a spider!" I screamed. "Get it off!"

"A little jumpy, Gabe?" Sari asked, wiggling her fingers at me. That's when I realized she had been tickling my neck.

I shot her a dirty look. Leave it to Sari to play a joke at a time like this.

"Sure I'm jumpy," I snapped. "You heard that guy Shafik. What if he's right? What if there is a curse? What if we go inside the tomb and someone dies?"

"Yeah." Sari laughed. "And that was a real spider crawling on your neck."

"Shh!" It was Nila. She nodded toward Uncle Ben. He was busy working on the seal and needed quiet.

I stood by Uncle Ben and peered at the seal. Somehow the lion looked different in lantern light. His jaws looked more powerful. His lips were pulled back in a sneer. The glow seemed stronger. Brighter.

Behind the lion I could see the outline of a huge door. It looked ancient. Heavy. Hieroglyphics covered the dark wood.

Uncle Ben hammered softly at the seal. Then he tried to pry it open. The lock didn't break or even crack.

Uncle Ben pushed harder. He used more strength. Then even more. The seal was giving way!

He stopped.

"We're about to enter the tomb," Uncle Ben said in a serious voice. "A room no one has seen for four thousand years. Please stand back."

I held my breath. This was really it. What everyone had been working toward. Waiting for.

Uncle Ben knocked off the seal. The heavy lock fell to the floor. Everyone stopped breathing. But nothing happened. The door didn't swing open. It didn't move an inch.

We all sighed, disappointed. There was more work to do.

Crack! The wall next to the door suddenly split down the middle like a broken egg.

"How did that happen?" shouted Uncle Ben. "That's a solid stone."

Crack! The rock exploded into two huge jagged pieces. *Whoosh!* Sand poured out of the wide crack. We stood frozen in a panic, as still as statues. More sand streamed through . . . and more . . . and more.

"It's a trap!" Uncle Ben shouted above the roar. "To catch grave robbers!"

A loud creaking noise filled the chamber. The ancient door! It was sliding open!

Uncle Ben lifted the lantern high. "Come on!" he ordered. "Into the tomb!"

"Into the tomb!" I echoed. My heart pounded as we slogged through the heavy sand. I quickly stepped through the doorway.

I heard the sand slow to a trickle behind us. A second later it stopped.

"Whew!" Uncle Ben said when everyone stood in the room with him. "I thought we were going to be buried in sand!"

My heartbeat slowed to normal. I looked around to check out the new chamber. What dangers did it hold? What would happen here?

Nothing. There was no mummy. No treasure. Not even a cobweb. The room was totally bare.

"Oh no!" Sari moaned, seeing the empty space.

"Why isn't there anything here?" I asked, disappointed.

"It's another trick," Uncle Ben said. "That's all. This is a false tomb."

Sari edged closer to me. "Maybe we have to say the magic words, Gabe," she said softly. "And the prince will come to us.

"Kahru, Kahra, Kahri," Sari chanted.

"Sari! Stop!" I whispered.

Sari laughed. "What's the matter, Gabe? Are you afraid of a mummy? Scared it's going to come to life?"

"Yes!" I wanted to shout. "Yes, I'm afraid!" But I'd never tell Sari that. Not if a million trillion mummies marched right up to us.

"Kahru, Kahra, Kahri. Come on, Gabe," Sari demanded. "Are you chicken?"

I knew she would start clucking any minute.

"Of course not," I insisted.

"Well then, say them," Sari whispered again. "Say the ancient words."

"Kahrukahrakahri," I said in a rush. "Happy?"

The lantern suddenly flicked off and on.

Sari and I both leaped over to Uncle Ben. "Wh-wh-why did the lantern do that?" I stammered.

"There may be some cracks in the wall," Uncle Ben replied. "Wind could be getting in."

I sighed, relieved. Of course there was an explanation. And calm, cool Uncle Ben knew what was going on. He'd never panic.

"Gabe!" Uncle Ben suddenly cried. "There in the wall. Look!"

I whipped my head toward the wall. A small white object sat lodged in a crack. The bundle was wrapped in bandages. I saw fingers. I shuffled closer.

"My summoner!" I shouted. "But I dropped it in the other room — in the spider pit. How did it get in here?"

I reached out to grab the summoner.

But the hand grabbed me instead!

"It won't let go!" I screamed. "Aahhh!"

"Is there really a mummy in here?" I asked my uncle Ben as we entered the pyramid.

Uncle Ben warned my cousin Sari and me to stay close while we searched for the tomb of Prince Khor-Ru.

Before I knew it, I fell into a deep, dark pit. In the pit, there was a beautiful lion's head—and a terrifying cobra inside!

Quickly, Uncle Ben and Sari lowered a rope into the pit and pulled me up to safety.

"That's the seal of Prince Khor-Ru!" Nila, a newspaper reporter, exclaimed that night, when I showed her a picture of the lion's head.

The next morning Nila returned to the pyramid with us to open the tomb.

Sari made me say the magic words—"Kahru Kahra Kahri." I did—and a mummy's hand reached from the stone and grabbed me!

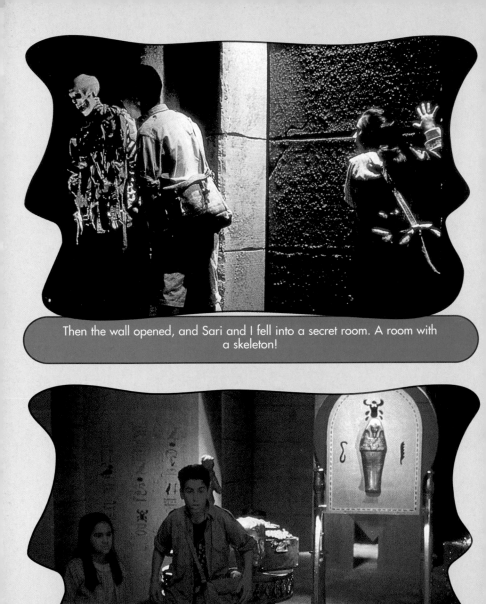

Then the wall opened, and Sari and I fell into a secret room. A room with a skeleton!

But we found Prince Khor-Ru's tomb and his golden treasures.

Sari and I decided to open the mummy's case to take a peek at him.

But we didn't know that the mummy was standing right behind us.

And we didn't know something else—that Nila was a real Egyptian princess with an ancient secret!

7

The summoner grasped my wrist tightly. "Hey!" I yelled. I pulled and twisted. But I couldn't get away. The hand had me in a grip of steel.

"It won't let go!" I screamed in terror. "Help! Uncle Ben!"

The hand clamped down. Tighter. Tighter. It squeezed my wrist. Sweat poured down my face. Why couldn't I get free? Why wasn't anyone helping me?

I saw Sari stroll toward me. "Give us a break, Gabe. You're just getting back at me. You're playing some dumb trick."

I could see Uncle Ben watching us, smiling. He thought I was joking, too.

The hand pinched me hard.

"Help!" I squeaked. "Nila!" I was in pain.

The look on Nila's face changed. She understood. Finally!

"Oof!" The hand yanked me back against the wall.

I tasted dust. "Agh!" I coughed.

"Gabe's not kidding!" Sari cried. She ran over, grabbing my arm. Then she tried to pull me away from the summoner.

"Ouch! My arm is breaking!" I yelled. But Sari's pulling didn't do any good. I was stuck fast.

"Gabe!" Sari sobbed in my ear.

Uncle Ben raced over. Before he reached us, the stone wall began to spin around. It turned like a revolving door, pushing Sari and me with it.

Uncle Ben couldn't stop fast enough. The spinning wall hit him in the head. "Ow!" he sputtered. He dropped to the ground.

The wall kept turning. It twirled us away. Away from Uncle Ben. Away from Nila.

Into darkness.

The summoner suddenly let go of me. I collapsed on the ground.

Sari fell right behind me.

"Gabe?" Sari said, confused. She rubbed her head. "What happened?"

I stood up slowly. "The wall swung around. . . ." I squinted into the dark. "It pushed us into another room. And now we are sealed off —"

Sari understood in a flash. She jumped up from the floor. "Help!" she shrieked. "Get us out of here!"

Her shouts echoed through the room. And then there was quiet.

I felt my way along the wall. I was frantic. There had to be some kind of opening. Some secret way to get back to the other chamber.

There wasn't. The wall felt smooth to the touch.

"This room is closed up tight," I said with a moan. I kept moving along the wall, checking it out. There had to be a door.

At last my hand brushed up against something hard. Something curved and knobby.

Definitely not cool, smooth stone.

My eyes got used to the dark. I could see some kind of shape now. I picked the object up. Maybe it was a secret switch for the door. Whatever it was, I clutched it.

In the dim light I tried to see what I was clutching. White lines glinted back. I looked closer. I squinted harder.

Finally I realized what I was looking into.

Two hollow eye sockets stared straight at me.

It was a skull!

"Yow!" I yelped, dropping it to the ground.

Sari started to scream again, too. "Dad! Nila! Help!"

I shouted with her. "Uncle Ben! Help us!"

Silence.

"It's useless!" Sari cried with a groan. "These walls are too thick. They can't hear us."

She shifted closer. I could actually feel her shudder. "We may never get out of here."

Sari was right. We'd be stuck there forever. No food. No water. Our flesh would rot.

It would drop from our bones in patches. In the end, we'd be skeletons, too.

I shook my head to clear it. We couldn't give up!

"We have to try and escape," I urged Sari.

Once again I examined the wall. I made my way along, hand over hand.

Hey! I felt something. A small crack. Then a longer, larger one going down to the floor. A rush of wind blew through.

"Sari!" I cried. "There's a way out!"

It wasn't the way we had come in. And who knew where it would lead. But it was worth a try.

Sari raced over, quick as lightning.

"I'm going through," I said, determined.

Sari touched my arm. "Be careful," she whispered.

I sucked in my breath. Then I squeezed through the narrow slit.

I was in another chamber. The air felt different. Colder. As if there was a lot of space around me. The room must be huge, I thought. But it was too dark to see.

Sari stumbled in behind me. She grasped my arm tightly. I had no idea what to do next. Oh, why isn't Uncle Ben here? I thought to myself. He'd know where we are. He'd know what to do.

A creepy feeling hit me in the stomach. I felt a pair of eyes on us. Watching. Following our every move. I whirled around.

Then I froze.

Glowing red eyes gazed at me from across the room.

8

I couldn't stop staring at the glowing eyes. I stood rooted to the spot.

Sari saw the eyes and shrieked.

That broke the spell. I crept forward. I had to get closer. I had to see the creature behind the red eyes.

Inch by inch I drew nearer. Then I spied a golden mane. A snarling mouth. A lion!

Was it just the lion's head seal again? No!

This lion sat atop a golden throne. His eyes were bright red rubies, gazing back at me.

"Whoa!" I breathed. The sight was totally incredible.

Sari hopped with joy. She forgot her fears.

"This is it!" she cried. "We found the prince's tomb. This is his throne!"

The tomb! We'd found it for real this time.

Everything came slowly into focus. We saw clay pots in perfect shape. There wasn't a scratch on them. Ancient chests stood scattered about.

I tugged open one drawer. Piles of colorful jewels spilled out. I pulled open another drawer. Gold cups and bowls and plates glistened softly.

Treasure! The room was filled with treasure!

I felt almost dizzy. Overwhelmed by it all. Then I remembered we had no way out of the tomb.

"Great," I muttered. "We'll be the world's richest skeletons."

"Gabe!" Sari called. "Look at that wall!"

I reeled around. A tall mummy case stood against the far wall. It had to be the prince! He was here, just as Uncle Ben had hoped.

Sari and I gripped hands. We edged closer

to the case. Our footsteps echoed on the stone floor.

I gaped at the looming mummy case. It must have been eight feet long. Rectangular like a coffin, but with curved shoulders. A human face was carved on the lid. We stood close enough to see the bright paint. Not one piece was chipped.

No one had seen it in four thousand years. We were the first. Sari wanted to be the first to feel it, too. She stretched out her hand.

"What are you doing?" I whispered.

"I'm going to open it," she said firmly.

I swallowed. "But . . . what if it wakes the prince?"

Sari rolled her eyes. "Don't you want to be the first to see him?" she demanded.

"Sure," I told her. "I just don't want to be the last."

Sari pulled at the lid. "Are you going to help or not?"

I sighed. Of course I'd help. I couldn't just stand around watching.

I gave a hard shove. But the lid was heavy. No way would it budge.

Something on the floor scuttled past my feet. I peered down. Was it one of those beetle things? Like the scarab I wore around my neck?

I didn't like being in the prince's tomb. Not one bit.

"Come on," Sari ordered. "Don't stand there staring at the floor."

I put my shoulder to the lid and shoved. The lid moved.

"Work it back and forth," Sari said through gritted teeth.

We kept pushing and pulling. Finally Sari said, "Now! With all your might!"

We heaved. The lid sprang open. I jumped back. But the coffin was empty. Dark wood stared back at us.

"Nobody home," I said, relieved.

Then we heard it. *Shush, shush, shush.* A soft, scraping noise behind us.

"What's that?" Sari asked.

"I don't want to know," I answered.

SHUSH, SHUSH, SHUSH.

The noise grew louder. It filled the room. We turned around. We had to. And there it was.

The mummy.

9

The prince's mummy lurched across the room. He dragged tar-stained bandages across the floor. His eyes bored into mine.

The mummy staggered. He held up his arms, stiff as boards.

I couldn't move. Sari stood beside me. She barely breathed. The mummy jerked nearer.

He swiped at the air in front of us. His bandages crackled and tore. Sari gasped.

A voice suddenly cut through the room. "Come to me," it ordered.

Was it the mummy speaking?

"Come to me!" the voice repeated. It sounded familiar . . . as if I had heard it just moments before.

It wasn't the mummy. It was Nila!

She had found the entrance to the room. She wore ancient ceremonial robes and big clangy jewelry. She looked like a princess.

"Nila!" I choked out.

"Come to me," she ordered fiercely. She fixed her gaze on the mummy. "Come to me, oh my brother."

At her words, the room burst into light. Torches lined the walls.

The mummy shuffled forward. His brittle bones creaked.

Nila continued talking to the prince's mummy. "It is Princess Nila, your sister. I have waited so long for this day. Now we are together."

She lifted her arm.

"Hey!" I shouted. "You're holding my summoner!"

"Silence, foolish one!" Nila commanded me. "You own nothing. The summoner is mine."

The mummy creaked forward. "Now we shall rule this land again," Nila told him. "Just as we did four thousand years ago."

"She's crazy," I whispered to Sari.

Nila heard me. She smiled wickedly. "Have you stopped believing in the summoner?" She spat out the words. "The summoner was the only thing that could awaken my brother. The words were not enough."

Nila suddenly turned to the mummy. "Destroy them, my brother!" she cried. Her face glowed in the torchlight. "There can be no witnesses!"

I thought we were finished. But the mummy did not obey Nila. He thudded across the room . . . past us . . . right to Nila instead. In one jerky move, he ripped the pendant from her neck.

Nila gasped and dropped the summoner to the ground.

"Let. Me. Rest. In. Peace," the mummy croaked. He held the necklace high in the air.

Nila paled. "Khor-Ru," she quavered. Then she made her voice firm. Loud. "You were weak. Lazy. I was strong. I was the one who ruled. Do you remember, oh my brother?"

"I remember." The mummy lowered his arm.

Nila smiled. She thought she had him. But the mummy turned and threw the pendant against the wall. It shattered to bits. Shards of amber were sprinkled over the floor.

Nila twitched in pain, "Ahhh!" she sobbed. "My life is over!"

She fell to her knees. She tried to scrape up the slivers of amber.

It was useless. The pendant was destroyed.

"I lived inside that stone," Nila moaned. "Every night. For four thousand years. And now ... oh ... I'll never ..."

A jolt of pain hit Nila hard. She tried to get up. But something like white-hot lightning streaked through her body. The room blazed with energy. I couldn't see a thing. Blasts of wind whipped my clothes and hair.

What was going on?

The light faded. The wind died down. All was quiet.

And Nila was gone.

10

The mummy stood still as a statue. Nila's clothes lay in a heap on the ground nearby. A beetle crawled out of her sleeve.

"Nila?" I whispered. "Is that you?"

The beetle scuttled into the darkness.

"What about the mummy?" Sari hissed. "Is he —"

Creeeak! The mummy swiveled around.

"Dead?" I croaked. "Guess not!"

The mummy plodded toward us. "Do something!" Sari screamed.

I dashed to the pile of clothes. Then I flung them aside. The mummy wobbled after me. But I had what I wanted.

The summoner.

I waved it wildly in the air. "Stop!" I shouted. "Halt. Uh. Halteth!"

The mummy kept coming. He reached out for me . . . for the summoner.

"K-Kahru, Kahra, Kar-something or other," I stammered as I backed away.

The mummy lunged forward. He grabbed for the summoner. I stumbled away, and he missed.

Again he thudded closer. I edged up against the wall. There was nowhere to go. Nowhere at all.

The mummy lifted his bandaged arm. A musty, dead smell slapped me in the face. He leaned close.

Then I felt a strange heat. But it wasn't the mummy. It was the torches on the wall beside me.

The mummy grabbed my arm. With my free hand I tossed the summoner into the blazing torch.

"Nooooooo!" The mummy dropped my arm

as the summoner burst into flames. He lifted his hands as if in prayer. A low groan rumbled in his throat.

Then we heard another rumble. A different one. Loud and strong.

It rocked the entire chamber.

Earthquake!

I raced to Sari and grabbed her hand. "Run!" I shouted.

The floor cracked beneath us. Rocks and dirt fell from the walls. The tomb shook and quaked.

We had to get out!

A wall suddenly cracked open. "Through here!" I yelled to Sari.

Sari darted through ahead of me. I saw the mummy stumble to his feet. He eyed me evilly. His mouth turned down in a sneer.

"Hurry, Gabe!" Sari called.

I started to squeeze through the opening in the wall. My head went through. My shoulders and chest. But that was all. I was stuck!

I could feel the mummy tugging at my legs!

"Gabe!" Sari shouted. She pulled as hard as she could, and finally I was free.

We were outside the prince's tomb. But where exactly?

"Dad!" Sari cried. Uncle Ben lay on the floor in front of us!

He moaned. We knew he had been knocked out by the wall. He was just waking up! He seemed okay. We helped him to his feet as the pyramid began to tumble down around us.

"Ooohhhh!" the mummy moaned. He was trying to push through the wall opening. The crack grew wider. Out came the mummy's arm. He reached for Sari. He almost caught her by the hair.

Boom! The ceiling of the tomb collapsed. We heard one last moan from the mummy. And that was all.

"Follow me!" Uncle Ben shouted. And as the walls caved in behind us, we raced out of the pyramid.

It was nighttime. I sat on the floor of my tent. My suitcase lay open. Sari watched me throw things in one by one. I was ready to leave Egypt.

"Hey!" Sari dangled the amber pendant. "Don't forget this."

"You keep it," I told her quickly. "It's something to remember me by."

Sari grinned. Then she tossed it in my suitcase. "Old Egyptian saying. When you get a lousy gift, you're stuck with it."

We heard loud voices outside the tent. "Excuse me," I heard Uncle Ben say.

The next minute he dashed inside. "What should I tell those reporters?" he asked us. "The truth?"

I stifled a laugh. "You're really going to tell them the mummy in the pyramid walked."

"And that his sister is a four-thousand-year-old beetle," Sari added.

Uncle Ben grinned. "You're right — anything but the truth!" Then he shook his head and hurried back outside.

Sari looked down at the ground. She actually seemed shy. "It's too bad you can't stay," she said softly.

"I wish I could," I told her. "But I would like to get home. You know, where the dead are really dead. Next year you can visit me. I'll show you the strange world of shopping malls."

I snapped my suitcase shut.

"You know what else?" I continued. "I'm not going to buy any more summoners at the airport."

I picked up the suitcase to go. I should have checked it one more time. But I didn't. And I'll always regret it.

Why? The summoner had crept out of the tomb. It had crawled into my tent quietly. Sneakily. Without anyone knowing.

The hand was back. Charred. Burnt. But still powerful.

And I was carrying it home!

GET Goosebumps

by R.L. Stine

☐ BAB45365-3	#1	Welcome to Dead House	$3.99
☐ BAB45366-1	#2	Stay Out of the Basement	$3.99
☐ BAB45367-X	#3	Monster Blood	$3.99
☐ BAB45368-8	#4	Say Cheese and Die!	$3.99
☐ BAB45369-6	#5	The Curse of the Mummy's Tomb	$3.99
☐ BAB49445-7	#10	The Ghost Next Door	$3.99
☐ BAB49450-3	#15	You Can't Scare Me!	$3.99
☐ BAB47742-0	#20	The Scarecrow Walks at Midnight	$3.99
☐ BAB47743-9	#21	Go Eat Worms!	$3.99
☐ BAB47744-7	#22	Ghost Beach	$3.99
☐ BAB47745-5	#23	Return of the Mummy	$3.99
☐ BAB48354-4	#24	Phantom of the Auditorium	$3.99
☐ BAB48355-2	#25	Attack of the Mutant	$3.99
☐ BAB48350-1	#26	My Hairiest Adventure	$3.99
☐ BAB48351-X	#27	A Night in Terror Tower	$3.99
☐ BAB48352-8	#28	The Cuckoo Clock of Doom	$3.99
☐ BAB48347-1	#29	Monster Blood III	$3.99
☐ BAB48348-X	#30	It Came from Beneath the Sink	$3.99
☐ BAB48349-8	#31	The Night of the Living Dummy II	$3.99
☐ BAB48344-7	#32	The Barking Ghost	$3.99
☐ BAB48345-5	#33	The Horror at Camp Jellyjam	$3.99
☐ RAB48346-3	#34	Revenge of the Lawn Gnomes	$3.99
☐ BAB48340-4	#35	A Shocker on Shock Street	$3.99
☐ BAB56873-6	#36	The Haunted Mask II	$3.99
☐ BAB56874-4	#37	The Headless Ghost	$3.99
☐ BAB56875-2	#38	The Abominable Snowman of Pasadena	$3.99
☐ BAB56876-0	#39	How I Got My Shrunken Head	$3.99
☐ BAB56877-9	#40	Night of the Living Dummy III	$3.99
☐ BAB56878-7	#41	Bad Hare Day	$3.99
☐ BAB56879-5	#42	Egg Monsters from Mars	$3.99
☐ BAB56880-9	#43	The Beast from the East	$3.99
☐ BAB56881-7	#44	Say Cheese and Die–Again!	$3.99
☐ BAB56882-5	#45	Ghost Camp	$3.99
☐ BAB56883-3	#46	How to Kill a Monster	$3.99
☐ BAB56884-1	#47	Legend of the Lost Legend	$3.99

GOOSEBUMPS PRESENTS

☐ BAB74586-7	Goosebumps Presents TV Episode #1 The Girl Who Cried Monster	$3.99
☐ BAB74587-5	Goosebumps Presents TV Episode #2 The Cuckoo Clock of Doom	$3.99
☐ BAB74588-3	Goosebumps Presents TV Episode #3 Welcome to Camp Nightmare	$3.99
☐ BAB74589-1	Goosebumps Presents TV Episode #4 Return of the Mummy	$3.99

❏ BAB62836-4	**Tales to Give You Goosebumps**	
	Book & Light Set Special Edition #1	$11.95
❏ BAB26603-9	**More Tales to Give You Goosebumps**	
	Book & Light Set Special Edition #2	$11.95
❏ BAB74150-4	**Even More Tales to Give You Goosebumps**	$14.99
	Book and Boxer Shorts Pack Special Edition #3	

--------------------- GIVE YOURSELF GOOSEBUMPS ---------------------

❏ BAB55323-2	**Give Yourself Goosebumps #1:**	
	Escape from the Carnival of Horrors	$3.99
❏ BAB56645-8	**Give Yourself Goosebumps #2:**	
	Tick Tock, You're Dead	$3.99
❏ BAB56646-6	**Give Yourself Goosebumps #3:**	
	Trapped in Bat Wing Hall	$3.99
❏ BAB67318-1	**Give Yourself Goosebumps #4:**	
	The Deadly Experiments of Dr. Eeek	$3.99
❏ BAB67319-X	**Give Yourself Goosebumps #5:**	
	Night in Werewolf Woods	$3.99
❏ BAB67320-3	**Give Yourself Goosebumps #6:**	
	Beware of the Purple Peanut Butter	$3.99
❏ BAB67321-1	**Give Yourself Goosebumps #7:**	
	Under the Magician's Spell	$3.99
❏ BAB84765-1	**Give Yourself Goosebumps #8:**	
	The Curse of the Creeping Coffin	$3.99
❏ BAB84766-X	**Give Yourself Goosebumps #9:**	
	The Knight in Screaming Armor	$3.99
❏ BAB53770-9	**The Goosebumps Monster Blood Pack**	$11.95
❏ BAB50995-0	**The Goosebumps Monster Edition #1**	$12.95
❏ BAB60265-9	**Goosebumps Official Collector's Caps**	
	Collecting Kit	$5.99
❏ BAB73906-9	**Goosebumps Postcard Book**	$7.95
❏ BAB73902-6	**The 1997 Goosebumps 365 Scare-a-Day Calendar**	$8.95
❏ BAB73907-7	**The Goosebumps 1997 Wall Calendar**	$10.99

- -

Slappy's eyes really light up!

It's Every Dummy's Dream!

Goosebumps®

Three books in one! Surprise!
An awesome cover with flashing eyes!
Get three of your all-time favorite stories:
Night of the Living Dummy #7,
Night of the Living Dummy II #31, and
Night of the Living Dummy III #40—
together in *one* hardcover book that
lights up when
you open it!

The Goosebumps Monster Edition #2

by R.L. Stine

Coming to a bookstore near you!